CINDERELLA LIBERATOR

Rebecca Solnit

WITH ILLUSTRATIONS BY

Arthur Rackham

VINTAGE

Chapter One

THE CINDERS

ONCE UPON A TIME there was a girl named Cinderella. She was called Cinderella because she slept by the fireplace in the kitchen of a great house and sometimes the cinders burned holes in her clothes. (A cinder is another name for a red-hot bit of wood from the fire.) Her clothes were old and worn and tattered.

She slept there because she was in the kitchen cooking and washing all day and because she did not have a bedroom. She did kitchen work all day because her stepmother made her do it. Her stepmother made her do it all, because even though there was plenty for everyone, and plenty of people to do the work, her stepmother believed there was not enough for everyone. And she wanted lots for her own two daughters, Pearlita and Paloma. (Nobody asked what Cinderella or Pearlita or Paloma wanted.)

Sometimes Cinderella was sad and wanted to go and play with other children. Sometimes she was happy to go to the market to buy eggs from the chicken lady and apples from the apple farmer and milk from the dairy farmer. Sometimes she liked making cakes with the apples and the milk and the eggs and flour from the wheat farmer. Sometimes she wanted to run away, but she was not sure where to go. Sometimes she was tired.

Cinderella became a good cook. She got to know everyone in the marketplace. She grew strong and capable. Pearlita and Paloma sat upstairs trying on clothes and arranging their hair and not going out, because the people in the town were not fancy enough for them, according to their mother.

Chapter Two

DRESSES AND HORSES

And then one day came the news that the king's son, Prince Nevermind, was holding a great ball, which is what they called dance parties in those days. The stepmother made sure that Pearlita and Paloma were invited, and they spent days trying on clothes and ordering dressmakers to make them new dresses out of satin and velvet and glitter and planning how to put up their hair and stick it full of jewels and ornaments and artificial flowers.

Cinderella came upstairs to bring them some ginger biscuits and saw all the piles of jewels and all the mirrors and all the fabric and all the fuss. Pearlita was doing her best to pile her hair as high as hair could go. She said that, surely, having the tallest hair in the world would make you the most beautiful woman, and being the most beautiful would make you the happiest.

Paloma was sewing extra bows onto her dress, because she thought that, surely, having the fanciest dress in the world would make you the most beautiful woman in the world, and being the most beautiful would make you the happiest. They weren't very happy, because they were worried that someone might have higher hair or more bows than they did. Which, probably, someone did. Usually someone does.

But there isn't actually a most beautiful person in the world, because there are so many kinds of beauty. Some people love roundness and softness, and other people love sharp edges and strong muscles. Some people like thick hair like a lion's mane, and other people like thin hair that pours down like an inky waterfall, and some people love someone so much they forget what they look like. Some people think the night sky full of stars at midnight is the most beautiful thing imaginable, some people think it's a forest in snow, and some people ...

Well, there are a lot of people with a lot of ideas about beauty. And love. When you love someone a lot, they just look like love.

Cinderella wished she could go to the ball, but she had nothing to wear apart from her everyday dress with the ashes and the patches and the holes. And she had not been invited.

There is nothing worse than not being invited to the party.

She went upstairs on the great day and helped Pearlita and Paloma pile up their hair with ornaments and put on their ballgowns, which were so long and tight they couldn't have run after a dog or climbed a fence. They were not sure they were beautiful, but they were sure that being beautiful would make them happy.

Off to the ball they went, in the family coach pulled by the family horses, and down went Cinderella to the kitchen, which was very quiet. She sat by the fire, feeling very sad and alone and staring into the fire, and cried three tears. It was so quiet you could hear each tear fall into the ashes with a tiny splash.

I wish someone would help me, she said out loud in the quiet.

Suddenly there was a knock at the kitchen door. She opened the big creaky door, and a little blue woman was standing on the doorstep. She had a big skirt, and a big nose, and a pointed hat, and hands like knobbly blue twigs, and she was holding a black stick in those knobbly hands.

May I help you? asked Cinderella, and the little blue woman said, *I came to help you! I am your fairy godmother. You wish to go to the ball at the castle; is that so?*

Yes, said Cinderella.

And then you shall go, said the fairy godmother, whose voice sounded like milk pouring into a glass and the wings of the pigeons.

She said, *You need a carriage. Run into the pumpkin patch and get a pumpkin.* Cinderella opened the kitchen door as she was told and ran out into the night and picked a big orange pumpkin from the garden, as heavy as she could lift.

The fairy godmother waved her wand, and the pumpkin became a glass coach that glittered in the moonlight – for it was a full moon night, and moonlight made the town look like a magical blue world of blue light and darkness like black velvet. The moon was reflected in the glass coach.

Oh, sighed Cinderella, and then she thought, *But you can't have a coach without horses*. It was as if her godmother heard her thoughts. *Get me six mice from the trap*, she said, and Cinderella wondered what she had in mind.

The trap was just a box that mice walked into when they smelled cheese inside, but they couldn't get out until Cinderella let them out. Cinderella would walk down to the river with the box of mice and let them go free where they couldn't nibble at the cakes and loaves she baked. This time she opened it at the kitchen door. The fairy godmother waved her blue arm, and the tiny legs and round bodies and long hairless tails of the mice began to change. Their legs and their necks grew long, the dainty little mouse feet with their tiny toes became horses' hard hooves, their coats became shiny instead of soft, and their round backs arched. They shivered and shouted and suddenly six dapple-grey horses stood there, with black manes and tails like black rivers, black muzzles as soft as velvet, and the same round black eyes and pricked-up ears the mice had, but no mouse whiskers. They were lively horses, and they stamped and snorted and switched their tails and tossed their heads, ready to go.

Cinderella was astonished. *Now*, said the fairy godmother: *We need a coachwoman.*

I will get the rat trap, said Cinderella. There was one big grey rat in it, and then with another wave of the same blue arm with the same black stick, the rat was no longer a rat. It was a coachwoman with grey curls in a beautiful white velvet suit with a velvet hat, who bowed to her and said, *Good evening, young lady.*

Now, said the fairy, *six lizards from the garden*, and when Cinderella brought them back in a flower pot, there was another wave of the wand, and six footwomen stood before her, in silver satin breeches and jackets, and the footwomen immediately began hitching up the horses.

Oh my, said Cinderella. *Did the lizards want to be footwomen?* (Footwomen stand at the front and the back of the coach and make it look very important and busy. They open doors and deliver letters and sometimes blow a little gold trumpet to announce your arrival or hold the horses' reins when the coach stops.)

For tonight, said the fairy godmother, *they are here to help you, because you have always been kind to the mice and the rats and never put out poison for them or traps that hurt them, and you have always smiled and said hello to the lizards when you went out to pick some lettuce or some raspberries.*

The coach is amazing. But I can't go in my rags, said Cinderella.

The fairy godmother said, *What rags?* and waved her stick, which was a magic wand, and giggled. Sometimes, being a blue-skinned fairy godmother was fun.

Cinderella looked down, and her patched, worn work dress had become a beautiful ballgown embroidered with birds and trees and crystals that looked like raindrops or tears. It was made out of silk and it sounded like water when she moved, and it looked like the sky at the end of the day, blue and then deeper blue and then so blue it was almost black, with pale clouds drifting by.

She looked like a girl who was evening, and an evening that had become a girl.

They call some dresses evening gowns, but this dress really was one, with clouds and the first stars coming out and a crescent moon somewhere in there, and a few birds flying across the hem, black and shaped like the letter W, in all that blue. The stars sparkled and the fabric swished when she moved.

I love this part of my job, said the fairy godmother and giggled again.

Oh, said Cinderella, as she was almost ready to get into the coach in her beautiful dress, *I am still barefoot.*

One more wave of the wand, another giggle, and her dirty bare feet were clean, and she was wearing slippers that, like the coach, were made of deep-blue glass. They were not very comfortable and made a lot of noise when she walked on hard floors or stones, but looked very special indeed.

Away they went – the six horses yearning to gallop, the coachwoman keeping them at a lively trot – through the town at night, hooves clattering on cobblestones, to the castle.

No one questioned who the late guest was when she pulled up in such a fabulous coach led by such a fine team of horses, and she went into the ball, and she danced – for she had learned to dance in the market square at the harvest festival and by watching her stepsiters' dancing lessons and sometimes dancing about the kitchen by herself when she was at work or dancing with the boy who delivered the mail or the girl who delivered the newspaper when they knocked on the kitchen door.

She danced with so many people to the beautiful music of three drums, four tubas, five trumpets, six violins, seven harps, eight guitars, and nine flutes, round and round the ballroom, all the people in dresses twirling around, so that if you saw them from above, they looked like whirling flowers in full bloom. The people in satin jackets and velvet breeches and brocade hats looked like flowers that had not yet bloomed but were still folded up like buds.

And then she danced with the prince, round and round and round some more.

Prince Nevermind had very nice satin breeches and a very nice smile, and they talked a little until he asked her who she was. She was afraid he might laugh at her or send her away in front of everybody, and she ran away before that could happen. That is, she sent herself away. As she ran, her shoes came off, and she grabbed one but left the other behind her on the ballroom floor. She did not want to tell him she was Cinderella from the kitchen in the town below the castle.

She ran out barefoot into the night, and jumped into her coach, and the coachwoman called out to the horses and the footwomen jumped up, and the horses galloped off with snorts and clattering hooves, and they were home before she knew it.

Chapter Three

LIZARDS

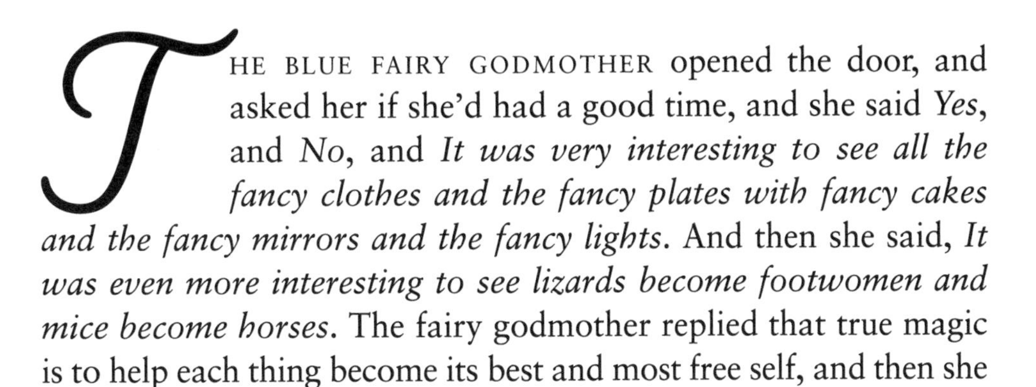

THE BLUE FAIRY GODMOTHER opened the door, and asked her if she'd had a good time, and she said *Yes*, and *No*, and *It was very interesting to see all the fancy clothes and the fancy plates with fancy cakes and the fancy mirrors and the fancy lights*. And then she said, *It was even more interesting to see lizards become footwomen and mice become horses*. The fairy godmother replied that true magic is to help each thing become its best and most free self, and then she asked the horses if they wanted to be horses.

Five of the horses said, in horse language, which fairy godmothers speak and most of us do not, that they loved running through the night and being afraid of nothing and bigger than almost everyone.

The sixth horse said she'd had a lot of fun but she had mice children at home and wanted to get back to them. The fairy godmother nodded in understanding, and suddenly the sixth horse shrank, and lost its mane, and its shaggy tail became a pink tail with a fine fuzz like velvet. And there she was: a tiny grey mouse with pink feet, running back to her tinier pink children in the nest in the wall to tell them all about the enchantment that had made her a horse for a night.

And then the lizards said, in the quiet language of lizards, that nothing was better than being a lizard, being able to run up walls and to lie in the sun on warm days and to snap up flies in the garden and never worry about anything except owls and crows, and though they loved wearing silver satin, and going to parties, and they had been happy to help Cinderella, and they would tell all their lizard friends about it, they would rather be lizards again. And suddenly they were, running off towards the garden on their little lizard legs, trailing long lizard tails, the moon making the scales on their lean lizard bodies shine like silver.

The coachwoman said she would be happy to stay a coach-woman, for her rat children had grown up and gone out into the world, and though she'd had many adventures as a rat, there were more adventures she could have as a coachwoman. And so she stayed in her velvet suit, and she led the horses off to the stable and gave them each a nice bucket of oats.

And Cinderella: she looked down at herself and said, *I have to make breakfast in a few hours, and I can't in this beautiful dress; I will spill something on it; it will catch fire; it will be in the way*. Suddenly she was all alone in her old patched dress, in which she could do anything, play with the dogs, climb the walnut trees, make the messiest cakes, garden where the lizards were basking in the sun. She might have thought she had imagined it all, but there was one blue glass slipper in her pocket, which she put in the kitchen drawer.

Chapter Four

FRIENDS

PRINCE NEVERMIND was a very polite person, and he was sad he had frightened his guest and she had lost her shoe. He had asked and asked at the party, but no one knew her name or where she lived, so the next day he got on his own fine black mare and rode about knocking on doors, asking if the person who wore that shoe was there.

No, said the people in the big brick house by the river, and *No*, said the people in the grey mansion on the hill, and *No*, said the people in the tower next to the woods, and *No*, said the farmer whose golden wheat fields spread on and on beyond her fine farmhouse, and *No*, said the clockmaker who lived in his little house full of ticking clocks, and *No*, said the painter in the house full of pictures of animals and places you only see in dreams (and her paintings), and *No*, said the dancing teacher in their house full of music, and *No*, said the blacksmith as she worked iron at her forge, and *No*, said the bird doctor as he fixed a sparrow's wing, and then the prince came to Cinderella's house.

Her stepmother answered the door and, greedy to see her daughters become friends with a prince, said that maybe the lost shoe was theirs. So the prince came into the parlour, and sat on the golden sofa, and one sister and then the other sister tried on the shoe, but their feet were too small, because when you sit at home all day and never run down to the river or carry home a full basket from the market, your feet don't grow strong and sturdy as they should.

Cinderella was bringing up the tea and the cake she had just baked when she saw the prince. Suddenly she was tired of so many things, of being in the kitchen, of not being at the table, of feeling like she was less important than her stepsisters, of not being invited to parties.

It is my shoe, she said. Everyone looked at her in surprise.

The prince handed it to her, and she pulled the other shoe out of her pocket (because all good dresses have big pockets), and put on the glass slippers, which had not disappeared when her dress had turned back into her everyday dress. Sometimes fairy godmothers forget a detail or two.

The two sisters ran out of the room in a tantrum – or two tantrums, one for each of them – because they believed they needed to be more important than their stepsister. Their mother had told them there was not enough for everybody and they needed to take things from other people to have enough for themselves. Which was, by the way, not true.

There is always enough for everyone, if you share it properly, or if it has been shared properly before you got there. There is enough food, enough love, enough homes, enough time, enough

crayons, enough people to be friends with each other.

After the stepmother had gone away, the fairy godmother appeared in a cloud of dark-blue dust. There was nobody in the room but the prince and Cinderella, and this blue woman with magic powers, but the prince hardly noticed the newcomer.

So, said the prince, *you are the girl who ran away. Why?*

Cinderella felt very embarrassed, but she said, *I was afraid. I am a servant and not supposed to go to balls and not supposed to have nicer clothes than my stepsisters.*

But her fairy godmother said, *You are the daughter of a great judge, who had to go far away to help others and thought his new wife and her daughters would be kind. You are the daughter of a great sea captain, who lost her ship at sea and will come home one day on another ship.*

And besides, said the fairy godmother, *nobody is good or valuable because of who their parents are, or bad because their parents are bad. They are as good and valuable as they are in their own words and deeds, and you are kind to mice and bake splendid cakes and have a heart full of hopes and dreams.*

What are your dreams? asked Prince Nevermind.

Cinderella said, *I would like to own my own cake shop, and I would like to be free to go and see the people on all the farms who raise the food I cook, and I would like to ride the dapple-grey horses, and I would like to see my mother come sailing into the bay on a fine ship.*

All those things seemed so far away. She felt sad for a moment, so she changed the subject. *What are your dreams?* she asked the prince.

He replied, after he thought for a moment, *I sometimes wish I was not a prince so I would not have people staring at me all the time and wondering why I have so much when they have not enough. I would like to wear the clothes the farm boys wear so I could play without someone shouting that I would get my satin breeches dirty. I would like to get dirty sometimes. I would like to be free to wander the hills all alone (I had to run away from my guards to find out who lost the shoe). I would like to learn how to make things grow and work so hard I sleep deeply all night, instead of doing nothing in the castle. I would like to have friends. Nobody is friends with a prince.*

I would like to have friends, said Cinderella. *I am friendly with all the people in the marketplace, and they tell me of their farms and lives and families, but I am not free to go and visit, because I must work every day here in the kitchen downstairs. That's why they call me Cinderella. Because of the cinders in the fire in the fireplace in the kitchen here.*

Well, said the fairy godmother. *Not all magic needs me. Perhaps you two are friends?*

I could use a friend, said the prince shyly, but bravely. *Would you like to be friends?* And then he felt terrible because maybe she would say no.

She did not say no. She said, *Yes, if you would too.*

And then the two of them stopped being people who had no friends.

Chapter Five

TRUTHS AND CAKES

The fairy godmother told Cinderella that she didn't actually have to stay there and work all day every day. That very day, she put on her boots and got on one of the dapple-grey horses, and the prince got on his black horse. They rode out to the apple orchard that belonged to the kind old apple farmer. There, they stood on ladders and picked apples until they were tired and they had thirty big baskets of apples. The old apple farmer promised to introduce the young prince to the neighbours, the other farmers. And he asked the prince to come back in the winter, when they cut back the branches of the apple trees when they are bare, and in the spring, when the trees are in bloom and the bees are all buzzing around.

Prince Nevermind rode home to tell his parents he wanted to be a farmer, not a prince, or maybe a farmer-prince, while the fairy godmother was waiting for Cinderella. *Go left until you get to the windmill, and then down the lane and up the alley, and you will find your cake shop. Next to it is a stable with five stalls and five dapple-grey horses inside, and the coachwoman lives above the horses.*

Why didn't you tell me I was free to go earlier? said Cinderella.

The fairy godmother said, *I was really busy helping some other children, and then I lost the directions to your house. Also, I am here to help people but they have to ask for help. You never asked for help until the night of the ball.*

(It is true that if you want or need help, it is really helpful to ask for it.)

Nowadays, Pearlita runs a hair salon where she piles up people's hair as high as it will go, and she's happy because she's doing what she loves. Paloma is the seamstress at a dress shop, where she makes dresses all day, because she discovered she liked making beautiful dresses even more than wearing them. They don't miss the days when they sat at home doing nothing and waiting for life to begin. They are good at what they do.

One day they went to Cinderella and said they were very sorry for how they had treated her, and that they were wrong, and could they be friends? Cinderella served them slices of cake, and later on Paloma made her some riding breeches, and then Pearlita brought over some hair cream for the horses' tails, and they were friends.

They became their truest selves, and so did their mother. Their mother, Cinderella's stepmother, turned into the roaring in the trees on stormy nights. Sometimes you can hear her outside, a strong wind rattling the windows and shaking the leaves off the trees, saying *More and more and more*, or *Mine, mine, mine*, and then the hungry wind dies down and she is gone until next time.

Sometimes that roaring is inside your own heart and head, and then it dies down there, too, the wind in all our heads that says we need more, we need to grab what someone else has and steal it away like the hungry wind. Everyone can be a fairy godmother if they help someone who needs help, and anyone can be a wicked stepmother. Most of us have some of that hunger in our hearts, but we can still try to be someone who says, *I have plenty*, or even *Here, have this* and *How are you?*

Cinderella runs a cake shop, and sometimes she sits with the people who come in to eat cake and drink a cup of tea and asks them what their dreams are, or what they would be if they could be anything they wanted to be, and what it means to be free. And then she listens, and sometimes she helps. She makes sure that everyone in the town has a birthday cake and goes to a lot of birthday parties.

Sometimes children running away from the wars in other kingdoms come to town, hungry and frightened and alone. Cinderella finds them, feeds them and puts them to bed in her attic until she finds other homes for them and gets them started in school. She always welcomes them back in the shop with a big slice of cake and a big hug. And as she grew older she became good at understanding the wars in people's hearts and helping them leave those behind, too. She isn't a fairy godmother, but she doesn't need magic to be a liberator – to be someone who helps others figure out how to be free.

Her mother the sea captain has come back and is proud of her. Her father the judge will be home one of these days, but her home will not be with that stepmother he was mistaken about. Someday she will get married, and so will the prince, but not to each other. Right now they are not old enough to get married, so we don't have to worry about that part of their story.

Besides, there is no happily ever after, only this bedtime story, and nighttime, and then tomorrow morning, and the day after that, and the day after that, and the spring coming after the winter, and the summer after the spring, and the earth going round the sun, and the lizards sitting on the wall in the sunlight, and the mice coming out in the moonlight to eat the cake crumbs.

A pair of glass slippers sits in the cake shop window, where they catch the sunlight too, but Cinderella wears solid boots in which she can stand at the counter or ride a dapple-grey horse out to see her friends.

Her friends include the farmer-prince, Paloma, Pearlita, the bird doctor, the dancing teacher, the painter and the clockmaker. They include all the people out on their farms where they grow the things the townspeople eat, and the girl who delivers the newspaper and the boy who delivers the post and the sailors in the harbour and her mother the sea captain in the house with the tower. And all the children in the town, who love her for her cakes and her kindness and her stories about what it means to be free.

But her friends don't call her Cinderella, because she doesn't wear a dress with holes burned by cinders and ashes anymore.They call her by her real name, which is

Ella.

AFTERWORD

Cinderella Metamorphosis

It began, as so many things do, with wandering in the public library. Mine has a used bookstore near the entrance, where I often browse, and one day not long ago I found a little print, a loose page from a broken book, for sale. It showed Cinderella as a cheerful barefoot girl in a ragged, patched blue dress, holding a huge orange pumpkin with both arms. I bought it, thinking I might eventually give it to a child, possibly to my magnificent great-niece Ella (and only while writing this story did I realize that without the cinders Cinderella is also an Ella).

Later on, I looked at the other side of this image from a book of fairytales. It had a bit of one version of the Cinderella story on it. And after the fairy godmother has turned mice into horses and the pumpkin into a coach, this interchange appears:

'Here, my child,' said the fairy godmother, 'is a coach and horses, but what shall we do for a coachman?'

'I will get the rat trap,' said Cinderella.

That passage, in which mice and rats change form, was striking, as was Cinderella's active collaboration in bringing about the metamorphosis. I realised that this was a story about transformation, not just about getting your prince. And about other relationships, including the one between Cinderella and the fairy godmother.

One thing led to another, and I decided to rewrite it for Ella (to whom *Men Explain Things to Me* is also dedicated) and began musing on possible mutations to introduce. The questions were how to preserve something of the charm of transformation and the plight of the child, and how to work out a more palatable exit from her plight than the one we all know.

Once I'd begun rewriting it, I began looking at illustrations and found and fell in love with the English illustrator Arthur Rackham's images for C. S. Evans's 1919 retelling of the story. Rackham is one of the great children's illustrators from the golden age of children's picture books, and he made images for everything from the classic fairytales to more contemporary children's books such as *Peter Pan* and *The Wind in the Willows* (and some pictorial editions of adult books, including *Gulliver's Travels* and *The Compleat Angler*). His colour work is often full of moody, drab colours and subtle tones, thickets, forests, tangled vegetation, delicate human, fairy, witch and animal beings who seem always to be turning, fleeing, striving, flying, reaching, twining like vines through the tinted spaces he set them in. The silhouettes are bolder and simpler.

I've always loved Rackham's work and am thrilled to share it with a new generation. Evans's retelling is sentimental and rife with ideas that virtue and beauty and upper-class status are more or less the same thing, and the least charming aspect of Rackham's images are the portraits of the stepsisters as preposterously awkward, ugly creatures, and we did not use those here. But there are other wonders and glories in his illustrations, aside from their sheer beauty. Silhouettes meant that the story might not feel so racially determined as the other images by Rackham (I was amused that some people first mistook the century-old images for those of the present-day black artist Kara Walker or thought they were rip-offs of Walker's more scabrous, scathing work with silhouettes – which is itself a conscious nod to the popular silhouettes of another era).

I was also touched by Rackham's image of the ragged child at work and thought of unaccompanied minors from Central America and immigrant domestic workers, who are a strong presence where I live, of foster children, and of all the children who live without kindness and security in their everyday lives, all the people who are outsiders even at home, or for whom home is the most dangerous place, or who have no home.

I liked the spirit of this silhouette-girl that Rackham portrayed. Even in rags she is lively, and she labours with alacrity, and runs and frolics wholeheartedly. She is stranded but not defeated. When it came time to write her story for our time, it seemed to me that the solution to overwork and degrading work is not the leisure of a princess, passing off the work to others, but good, meaningful work with dignity and self-determination – and one of the things the cake shop gives Cinderella, aside from independence, is the power to benefit others, because it's also a meeting place.

We are also in an age in which marriage is not how women determine their economic future or their identity, and so marrying the prince was going to have to go, too. Besides, the prince also seemed to need liberation. In the end, even the stepsisters needed to be set free, and if the stepmother was irredeemable, it's because she's all of us: insatiable craving and its underbelly, selfishness incarnate. She's who we all are when we feel poor amid plenty.

I wanted a story about liberation, about, as Keeanga-Yamahtta Taylor put it, 'how we get free'; or, as Buddhists sometimes put it, 'the liberation of all beings'. I wanted a kinder story, and I took from many other fairytales the theme about being kind to animals as a good thing to do because it's part of being a good person, but also a handy thing to do since they may return the favour. I wanted to set everyone loose to be their best and freest selves. It's why the book's title is *Cinderella Liberator*, a phrase that carries hints of Katniss Everdeen and Imperator Furiosa and the women of Hong Kong action films like *House of Flying Daggers* and *The Heroic Trio*, those powerful women who seize control of the means of production and destruction and move through the world like lionesses.

I wrote the story first for Ella, and then for anyone and everyone who loves the old stories in which mothers become trees and brothers become swans, in which animals hold conversations and girls open their mouths to speak and jewels and pearls spill out, in which magic models the work of transformation we all have to do for ourselves, on ourselves, all the time, and in which the huge tasks life sets us are clear and dramatic.

It's still for Ella and for her younger sister, Maya, and their mother, my first niece, Amanda. For Sam, Kat and Atlas, who love a good story; for Charlie, Elena, Berkeley, Dusty and Oscar, who were among the early readers; Ana Teresa Fernández, who was the very-first reader and whose powerful performance project in which she made Cinderella's shoes out of ice and wore them until they melted was a more ferocious rewriting of the story (a print of one of those ice shoes with her foot in it has the place of honour in my home; I have been living with Cinderella revisionism for a long time).

And it's for my grandmothers, Julia Walsh Allen and Ida Zacharias Solnit, both of whom were motherless girls, neglected, undereducated; neither of whom quite escaped that formative immersion in being unloved and unvalued; both of whom are long gone, though the repercussions of their devastation linger.

My maternal grandmother, Julia, whose immigrant mother died in childbirth, was raised by relatives in Brooklyn. Her education stopped in sixth grade, after which they made her work full time as a laundress while her girl cousins continued with their education.

My paternal grandmother, Ida, was an unaccompanied refugee child who, after years without parents, made it from the Russian-Polish borderlands to Los Angeles with her younger brothers when she was fifteen. There, her long-lost father and stepmother also treated her as a servant.

Their tragedies were a century ago and more, but this book is also with love and hope for liberation for every child who's overworked and undervalued, every kid who feels alone – with hope that they get to write their own story, and make it come out with love and liberation.[1]

---

1 'Cinderella' is a very old story, one version of a primordial story of the abandoned child who wins her way back to well-being (or, as the Aarne-Thompson-Uther Classification of Folk Tales has it, #510A, the 'Persecuted Heroine'). In 1892, Marian Roalfe Cox compiled a book titled *Cinderella: Three Hundred and Forty-Five Variants of Cinderella, Catskin, and Cap o'Rushes, Abstracted and Tabulated.* There are ancient Egyptian and Greek versions, a Chinese version from the ninth century with a magical fish and golden shoes, a twelfth-century French version, and various folkloric versions in Norwegian, German, Italian and other European languages. In the Norwegian version, a talking bull with magical powers takes the place of the stepmother; in the German 'Aschenputtel', a tree grows on the grave of the dead mother of the heroine and fills with birds, who aid her and give her a gold and silver dress – and later peck out the eyes of the stepsisters. In the Russian version called 'The Wonderful Birch', the tree that grows out of the mother's grave becomes the returning mother. There are violent and vengeful versions, versions with evil witches and no fairy godmother, annoying modern versions focused on marrying up, and dozens of new variations among children's books.

And now, one more, with gratitude to everyone who has taken the time to read it.

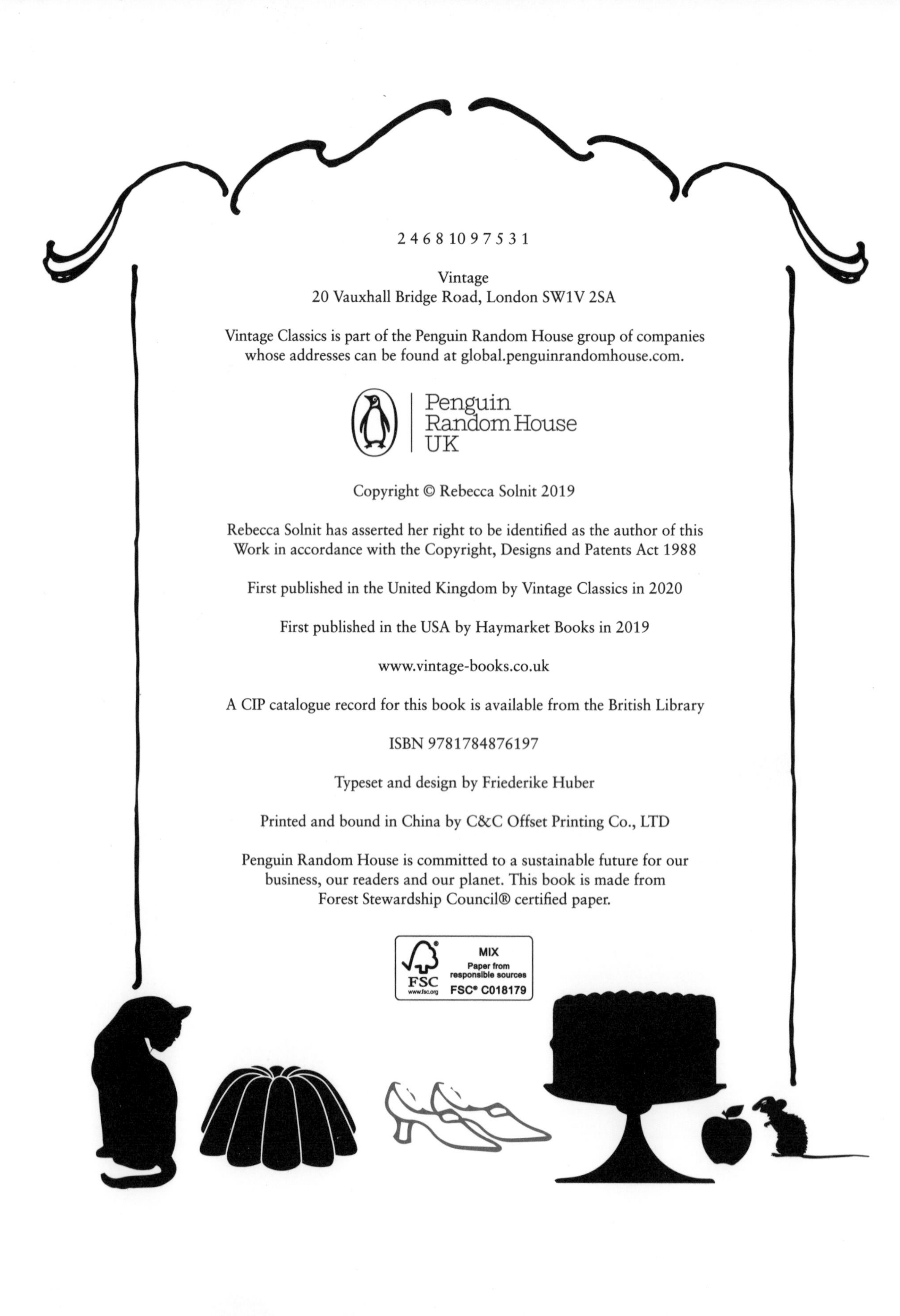

2 4 6 8 10 9 7 5 3 1

Vintage
20 Vauxhall Bridge Road, London SW1V 2SA

Vintage Classics is part of the Penguin Random House group of companies
whose addresses can be found at global.penguinrandomhouse.com.

First published in the United Kingdom by Vintage Classics in 2020

First published in the USA by Haymarket Books in 2019

www.vintage-books.co.uk

A CIP catalogue record for this book is available from the British Library

ISBN 9781784876197

Typeset and design by Friederike Huber

Printed and bound in China by C&C Offset Printing Co., LTD

Penguin Random House is committed to a sustainable future for our
business, our readers and our planet. This book is made from
Forest Stewardship Council® certified paper.